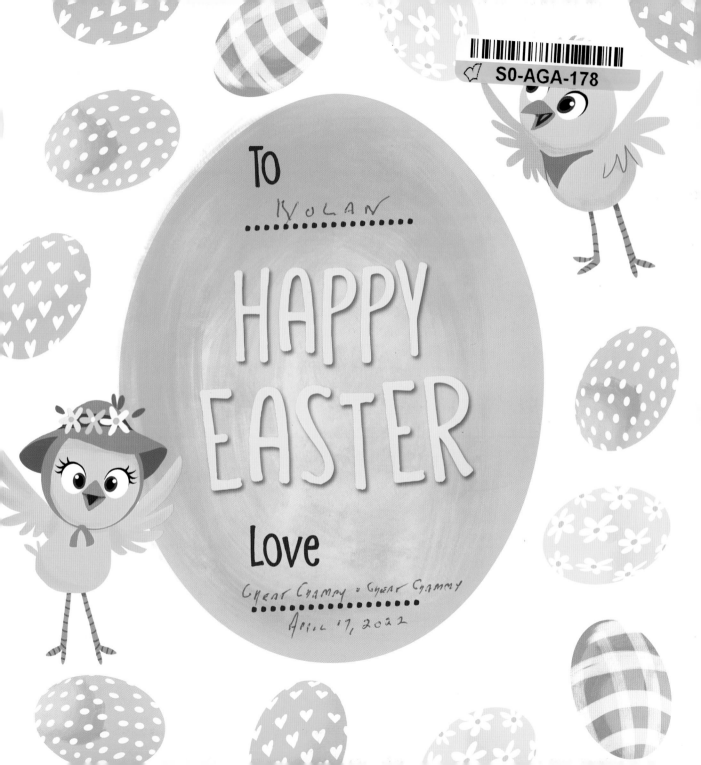

TO

Nolan

HAPPY
EASTER

Love

Great Grampy & Great Grammy

April 17, 2022

THE EASTER BUNNY
is coming to
WASHINGTON

Written by Eric James   Illustrated by Mari Lobo

sourcebooks
wonderland

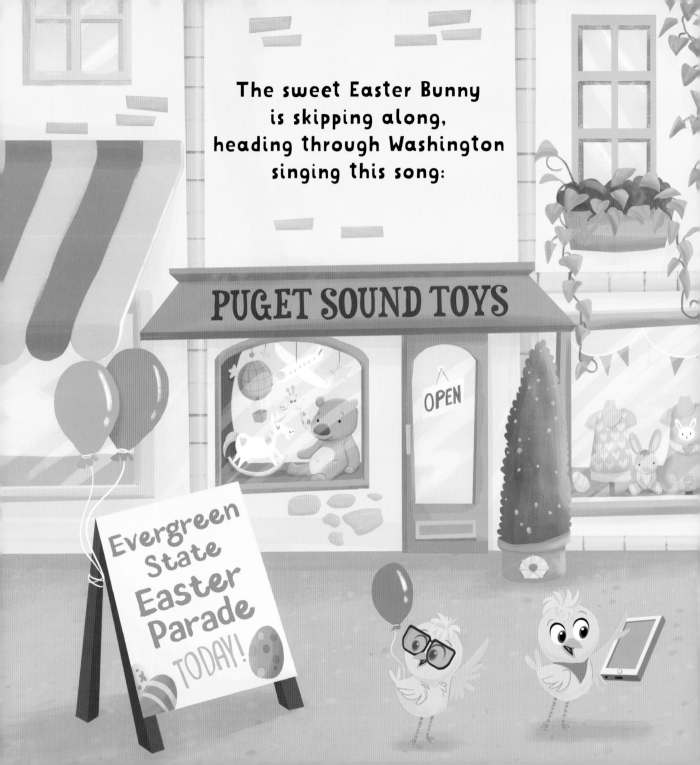

The sweet Easter Bunny
is skipping along,
heading through Washington
singing this song:

PUGET SOUND TOYS

OPEN

Evergreen
State
Easter
Parade
TODAY!

Cakes

BAINBRIDGE
ISLAND BOOKS

TINY THE
Washington
EASTER BUNNY

The Littlest
Bunny in
Washington

"The eggs are delivered.
My Easter job's done.
And now it is time
that I joined in the fun!"

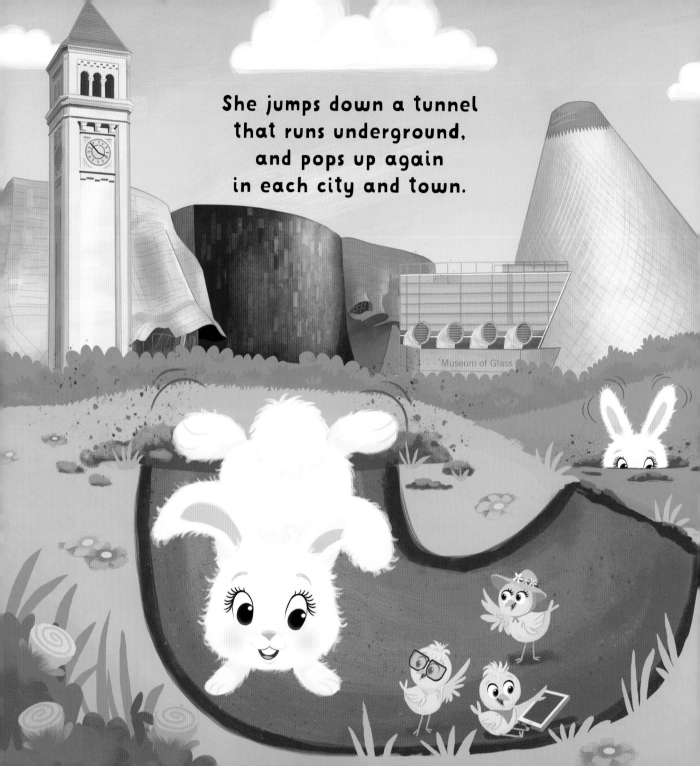

She jumps down a tunnel
that runs underground,
and pops up again
in each city and town.

Museum of Glass

THE MUSEUM OF FLIGHT

Walla Walla, Kent,
Vancouver, too.
I bet there's a tunnel
that's very near you!

In **Olympia** young children
have smiles on their faces,
and eggs decorated
like people and places!

WILLOW
GOLDFINCH
PARK

But one little boy
drops the egg from his hands.
A loud **CRACKING** sound
can be heard as it lands.

"Oh dear!" says the bunny,
and dabs at a tear.
"You need cheering up
so thank goodness I'm here!"

She wiggles her ears,
she hops on the spot,
she waggles her tail,
and he giggles a lot!

In Everett, there is
an Easter parade.
Most children are clapping
but one looks afraid.

That clapping is noisy.
These legs are so TALL!
It's crowded and loud,
and she's ever so small!

"Gee whiz, what a din!
I know just what to do.
Come here little one
and I'll hold hands with you!"

She wiggles her ears,
and spins her around.
The little girl laughs
as her feet leave the ground!

Down in Seattle
while having a rest,
the bunny eats Loganberry Pie.
(It's the best!)

Across in the park
there's an egg-rolling race.
A small boy falls down
and he's now lost his place!

The bunny trips up
as she's going to help.
She falls down the hill
with an **OUCH** and a **YELP**!

YELP!

OUCH!

She's just a big blur
as she tumbles on past.
The boy runs to help her.
He's going so FAST!

FINISH

She wiggles her ears,
he can't (but he tries!).
They hop up and down
for they've just won first prize!

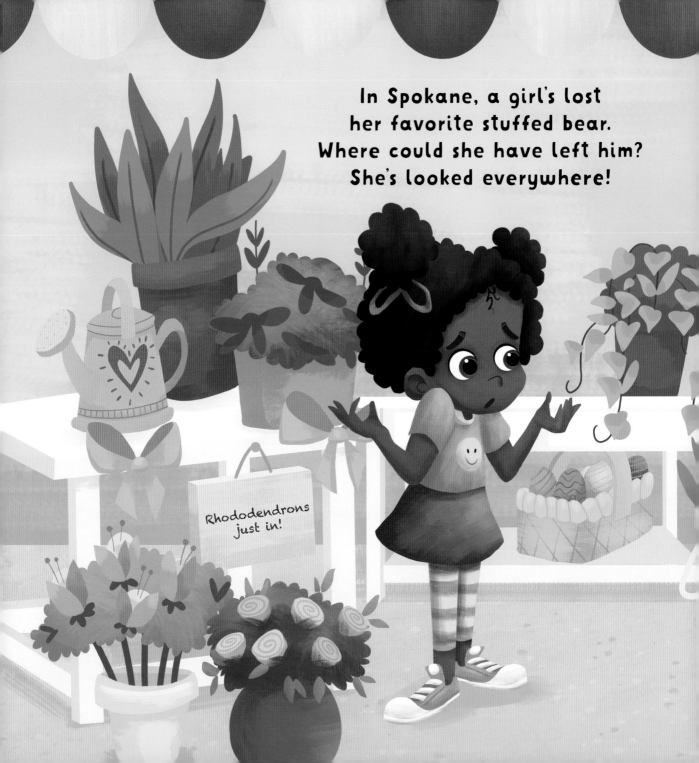

In Spokane, a girl's lost
her favorite stuffed bear.
Where could she have left him?
She's looked everywhere!

Rhododendrons
just in!

"When I'm feeling sad
do you know what I do?
I hop up and down!
Do you want to try too?"

She wiggles her ears, the girl thinks it's funny,
and laughs even more when she hops like a bunny!

They both jump around like they haven't a care.
And look what the chicks have just found, over there!

In Tacoma, the bunny
helps children with SHARING.

In Klickitat, she helps a sweet child
to be DARING.

In Bellevue she SINGS,
in Yakima she WIGGLES.

Wherever she goes
she brings LAUGHTER and GIGGLES!

This day's been so busy
but also such fun.
The bunny daydreams
in the warm setting sun.

The twilight is coming,
the three chicks are lazing,
and tweeting about
how this day's been #AMAZING!

The bunny jumps up,
snapping out of her daze,
"There's only three-hundred-
and-sixty-four days!"

More chocolate needs making!
New eggs will need wrapping!
It's all so exciting,
the three chicks start flapping!

"Washington's great
and we love being here.
We'll make lots more eggs
and we'll be back
next year!"

She wrinkles her nose,
she wiggles her ears,
she blows you a kiss,
and she just...disappears!

Written by Eric James
Illustrated by Mari Lobo
Additional artwork by Philip McIvor
Designed by Nicky Scott

Published by Sourcebooks Wonderland,
an imprint of Sourcebooks Kids
P.O. Box 4410, Naperville, Illinois 60567-4410
(630) 961-3900
sourcebookskids.com

Date of Production: August 2019
Run Number: 5015369
Printed and bound in China (1010)
10 9 8 7 6 5 4 3 2 1